TRUMPIANA

Patriotic Vernissage

by Ilya KATZ
President's political surrogate

ISBN 978-1-949720-41-9

Satirist is on God's side
And God is always right.

For author "America First"
is a Liberty at any cost.

If you care for some fun and enlightenment,
enjoy Ilya Katz satirical cartoons and writing.

Our President was nonstop
bombarded with negative cartoons
before his term and also during of his term.

Author is the first and only one
who decided to create something positive,
artistic and more truthful about our Leader
and he does it in humoristic genre.

As *JFK* stated:
"One person can make a difference
and everybody should try".
Professor Katz is doing very best
to stand up against democratic lie.

"Don't be scared, be prepared"

— Ronald Reagan.

America needs physically disabled members
in Congress.
Because they understand better other people's pain.

My goal is to bring electrical current
of naked truth dressed up in my satire
under chairs of so-called public servants.
So I decided to jump from my wheelchair
in *Debit* Wasserman Schultz, congressional chair.

If I will not strike with fire
If you will not strike with fire
If we will not strike with fire
Who will then dispel the liars?

Today author is on a noble mission
to bring Democrats hatemongers down
by degrading the false idols
to the level of the clowns.

Satirist's duty is to throw the truth
not only directly onto Democratic faces,
but also into their less honorable places.

The sharp satirical revelation
could give Democrats
diarrhea with constipation.

**President is fully equipped to fight
for what is right.**

Victorious leader couldn't be judged despite democ*RATS* lies and outrage.

They say "mind over matter".
Republicans do not mind
because Trump is a real matter.

Trump:
"Fight for Victory is not easy.
Let's keep ourselves busy".

Even on a Sun there are dark spots.
It doesn't matter Trump is much superior
than his contenders democrats.

Ronald Reagan is Trump's great ancestor,
and Donald Trump
is great Ronald Reagan's successor.

**Generation Z who is contaminated
with poison of socialism
need a preventive shot of American patriotism.**

**Mister President,
you will be a real St. Donald Trump,
if you clean bottomless Washington swamp.**

Donald Trump motto:
"America is an exceptional country
and I will do my best to keep it that way".

Run Donald, run!
Destroy fake media!
Have fun!

Donald Trump's socialism rejection
will bring him Victory in reelection.

Superman could stop a bullet with his chest.
Trump can put his enemies into a grave to rest.

**Trump's war chest
is the best!**

**Tomorrow, tomorrow...
Democrats will be very sorrow.**

A Republican: "Did you see the President
holding out an olive branch
of collaboration to you?"
A Democrat:
"Did you notice the big fist holding that branch?"

President offers work together with *CON*gress.
What will happen further - we can only guess.

God created President Trump not to be polite,
but sent him to fight
and to do what is right.

Napoleon conquered all the Europe,
but Donald Trump is not impressed.
He's sure and he is able
to conquer the whole world.

Trump: "I won't listen lefts,
I will not blindly follow rights.
I was born to lead,
God blessed my successful fight".

**Righteous has to possess a strong fist
to fight homegrown socialists.**

**President lost any patience
expecting from "do-nothing" *CON*gress
workable and real progress.**

**People support President Trump
when he is destroying the Washington swamp.**

Against democratic disorder
Trump fights with executive order.

Country will go following a Trump way,
hopefully it will be a fast moving highway.

President Trump knows how to make things done,
to achieve his goals and further run.

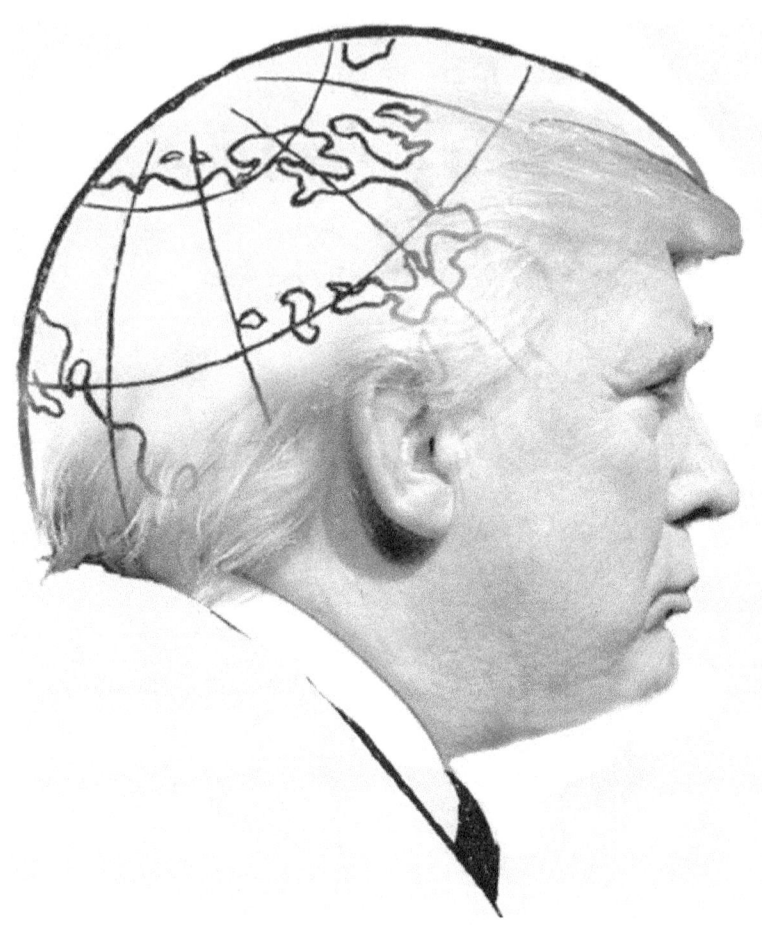

**In Trump's head is the whole world
so every country is begging for support.**

**Trump: "Our economy is on a real top,
Despite Democrats' fake predictions crap".**

**Trump: "Be persistent, have patience.
We are building
great future for next generation".**

Trump will get what he wants
from "do-nothing" CONgress.
Time to finish the wall on the border
and stop an immigration mess.

Donald Trump examined the Wailing Wall
in Jerusalem.
"A great wall", said Trump.
"We will build the same on the border with Mexico,
And let them cry".

**Trump's wall
is the defense for all.**

President Trump is not promising
to Americans pie in the sky.
He is standing fearlessly
against Democrats and their impudent lie.

President protects wealth of capitalism against deadly destruction by socialism.

America's winning economy
will perform to China
a lobotomy and a vasectomy.

**President Trump's dream
is to be a Winner-Supreme.**

**Xi Jinping, Chinese President
is a friend,
when he's ready to bend.**

Why is China President Xi Jinping hopping mad?
Because Donald Trump stomped on his balls.

Trump's "Art of the Deal":
obsession in progression.

Donald Trump believes it is possible
to cooperate with evil
if you're sure you can make a fool of him
but not vice versa.

**Trump's against China successful run
will not be an easy and will not be fun.**

**President Trump is trying hard
to save our dollar
from Chinese flood.**

In the end of the day
Trump will conquer Mexico and China
because their economies
will be in a deep vagina.

To curb a bureaucracy
President uses autocracy.

The government and people
are different civilizations.
Overblown bureaucratism
is detrimental to our nation.

The government employed 16,000.00 lawyers.
We also have in Washington 6,000.00 lobbyists.
So the President is bravely making a decision,
"It's time to perform parasites circumcision."

Trump: "No quid pro quo,
as it was no Russian collusion",
it's a nonstop idiotic democratic delusion.

There is an old saying:
"You reap what you sow".
America is a bountiful country.
We planted democrats in a power
and we will be harvesting a disaster.

Satirical KATZtus

**American Satirical Exceptionalism
refuses to digest antitrumpism.**

GALLERY OF TRUMP'S HATEMONGERS.

"Against the power of laughter nothing can stand"
- Mark Twain.

No apology for striking Democrats' pathology.

A satirist is on God's side
And God is always right.

A satirist who is not in opposition
is the same as soldier who left his position.

Satirical sharpshooting is an effective way to be heard.

Satirical laughter is the best medicine against vanity
and it is the most effective medicine
against swollen overblown authorities.

Who get so high that achieve political orbit
still vulnerable to gravitational power of satire.

The satirist is always right,
professor Katz is engaged in a fight.

"There is no distinctly american criminal class - except CONgress"

- Mark Twain

Nothing more dangerous than powerful idiots exploiting path of justice in opposite direction.

"We long for that most elusive quality
in our leaders-the quality of authenticity,
of being who you say you are,
of possessing a truthfulness beyond words."
- *Barak Obama Professional Humorist.*

Democrats and wishful impotents proclaim:
"Yes we can"
"Sorry, but you can't" - reply Republicans.

PEOPLE AND DEMOCRATS
ARE DIFFERENT CIVILIZATIONS.

To be "right" has two meanings.
One of them is "correct".
To be "left" also has two meanings.
One of them often follows the word "behind".

Free radicals endanger our life.
By the way, let us call them "ridicules".
Why consider them Liberals if they don't give
a damn about the liberty of the individual?
Why should we accept them as Democrats,
if they are deaf to the voice of the majority?
It may be proper to recognize them
as leftists, ideologically crippled left-brainers.

President's Donald Trump adversaries
will vanish very soon from the public horizon,
but author converts democratic fart
into immortal satirical art.

This is an ugly democRATic exhibition
of individuals guilty in democracy demolition.

Democratic presidential candidates
are qualified to participate
only in one process:
the digestive one.

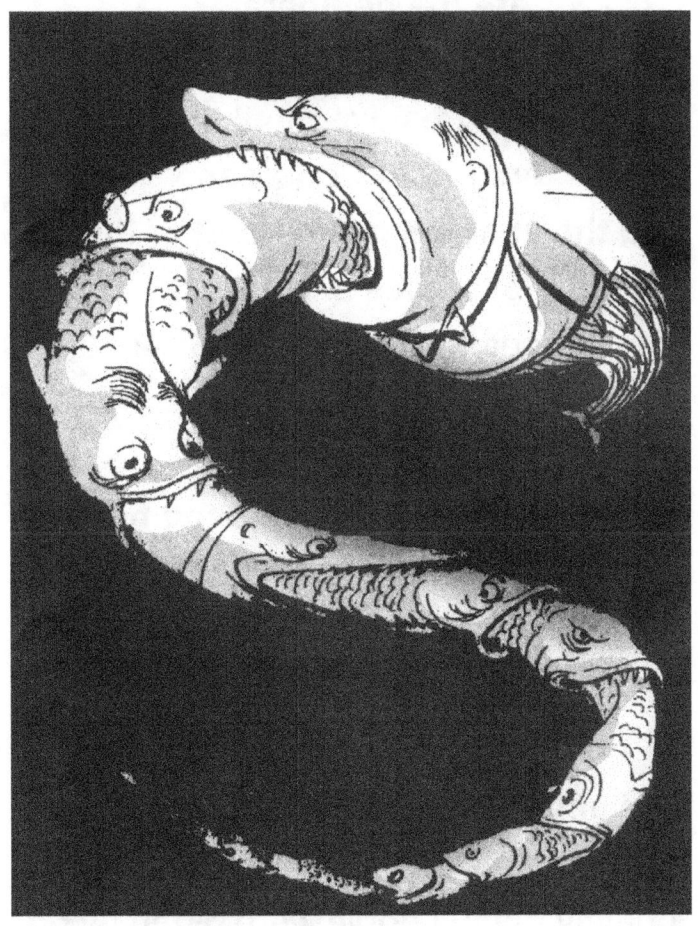

Democratic candidates swim in different styles
but will drown in the same way.

Undoubtedly,
the smartest people in the world,
the most progressive,
are the democrats.
And the smartest of the smartest,
the most progressive of all democrats,
are in the Congress.
And the absolutely smartest of them,
becomes a leader.
He passes around such ASSense,
That no one in the world can compete
with this person.
Please don't get your feeling hurt.
An ass otherwise called a donkey,
is the hard-earned symbol of the democrats.

If vampire will bite a human being
that person will become a vampire.
Unfortunately many people were bitten by donkey
and became a democrats

There is no leader in the Democratic Party.
The party reminds of a fly with a donkey's head,
which is able to move chaotically and buzz,
but not to fly.

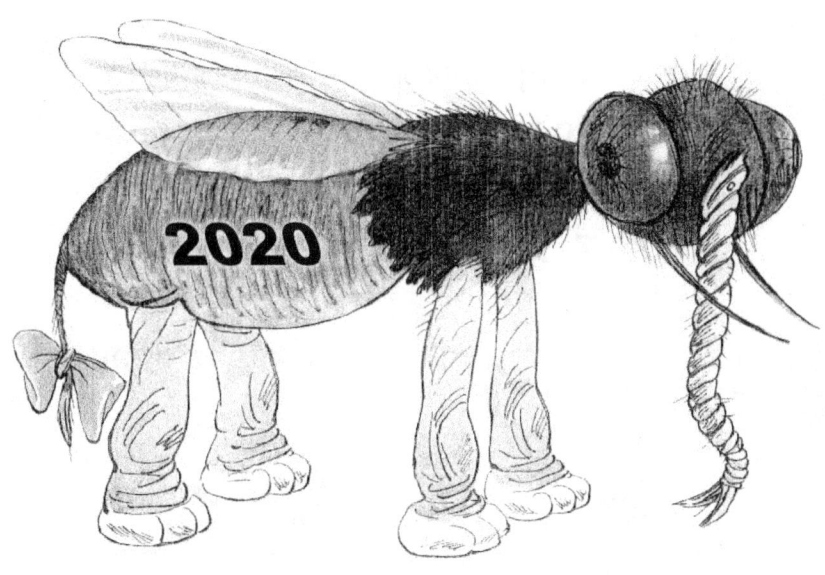

For Democrats, there is nothing more pleasant
than to discuss their future victories
while sitting up to the neck in sh@t.

Today Democ*RATS* are detrimental
to the whole, nation.
Why don't give them free contraceptives
to stop their multiplication?

Why don't delegate lawmaking in *CON*gress
to proctologist or gastroenterologist?
They will do it exactly the same
as mentally challenged Democ*RATS*
- through the ass,
but at least they will do it professionally.

How Republicans will get rid
of Democratic majority on *CON*gress?
Asking God to send asteroid
on the left side of the aisle.

The bearers of socialist infection,
Our modern zombies;
their activity resembles
The spread of infectious disease.

If Democrats derived from monkeys
it's understandable why monkey so humiliated.

SATIS*FICTION*

SATISF⚫CKTION

GUARANTEED!

From Socialist Loony

SOSialism is kingdom of parasitism

Obama is still alive, Obama is not dead.
Together with Democratic establishment
he shares the ideological bed.

Mr. Obama, Katz is on your back.

**If we want to damage this person's reputation,
it is enough, to tell the truth about him.
Why lie?
The truth is far more damaging.**

Barak is not rude, just cute.

I love you,
You love me,
I am your honey,
Please, send me money

Change never comes,
because Obama's promises were a sham.

It is untrue that Obama is only an incompetent person,
let's be objective he is dishonest as well.

Obama pours his ideological dregs
into the river of our society
and the public took it for new stream.

Those who brought Obama to power
got drunk from the drink of joy.
Later they paid back
with serious hangover and vomiting.

Obama's promises are similar to horizon.
The closer people are coming,
then further horizon is moving.

Idol worship is a reminder of slavery.
Hopefully soon the number of worshipers
will become negative.

Political xylophone,
Democratic Obama-phone has still not gone.

Naivety is a sister of stupidity,
deplorables don't believe in Obama's disability.

**The Democratic Party is in a hole,
and that hole is growing.**

Obama:
**"Let's discuss and resolve our political situation,
only Michelle is able to lead our nation".**

Obama to his very ambitious spouse:
"Try hard a little more
and we will be in a White House".

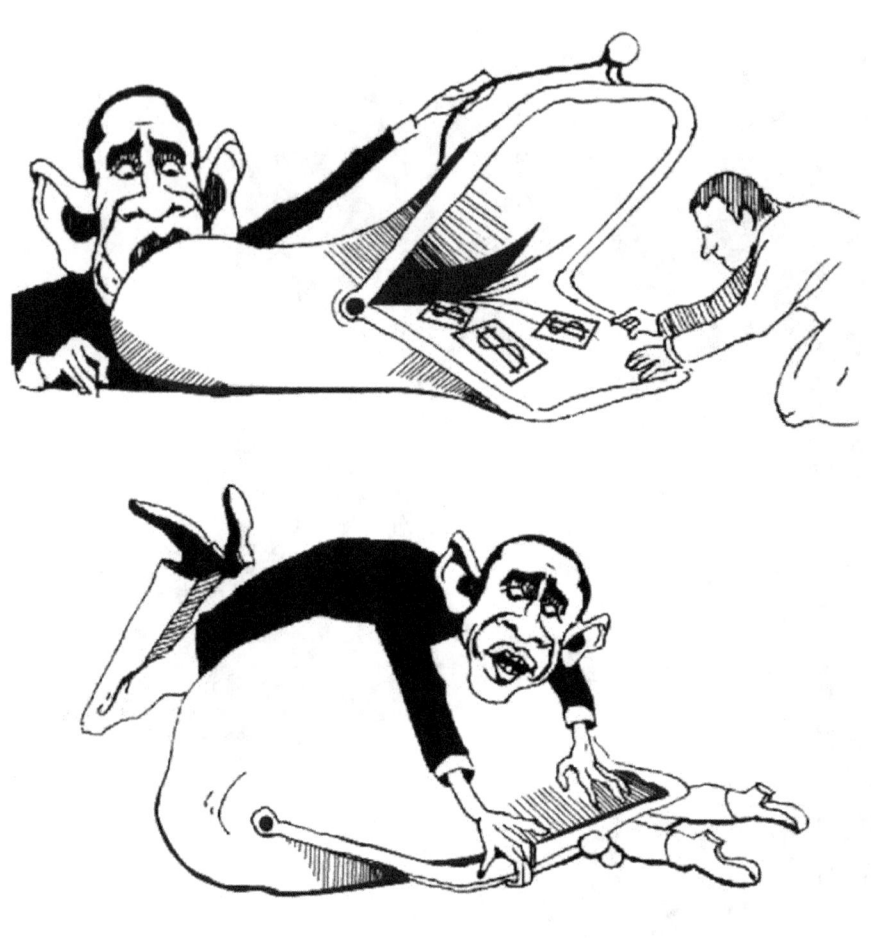

Don't pay attention to Democratic crap.
Freebies exist only in a merciless trap.

Taxaholic-in-Chief

**Music helps the work process,
soon discussion of Obama's outdated ideas
will be accompanied by Mozart's "Requiem".**

Obama is still armed with populist ideas and he is very dangerous.

Welcome to "democratic" political court.
Instead of common sense
people find an absurd.

Our impudent and indecent
fake mainstream press
is enjoying Trump's impeachment
from unconstitutional *CON*gress.

Same-sex marriage

**God will soon punish sins,
those indecent political twins.**

Schiff and Nadler try very hard
to squeeze the President
with false accusations fart.

This is the way as left press
brings to the Trump's family
torture and disgrace.

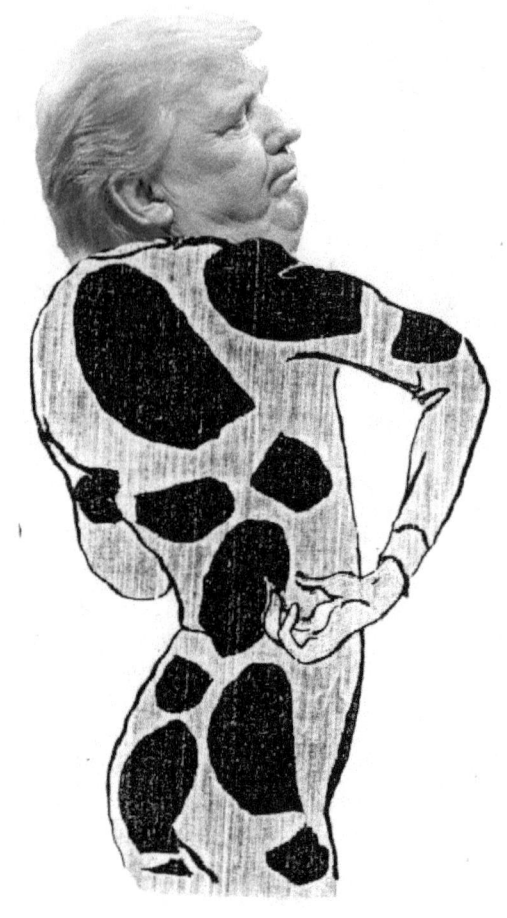

**Unfortunately Democrats never give up
insulting President Trump
by their malicious crap.**

"Don't worry, be happy!"

**Democrats are ready
to take care of President's rights
days and nights".**

It's ugly democratic experiment.
No more comments.

President Trump is doing well,
so he will survive the Washington hell.

**DemocRATs are doing "the best"
to lock President under arrest.**

**God damn *CON*gress put President
into a straight Jacket.
But "we the people" are not pleased
with such political racket.**

Democrats song: "Bye, bye liberty,
bye, bye bravery,
hello, slavery."

Failed dream of congressional democrats majority
is to gain over President's superiority.

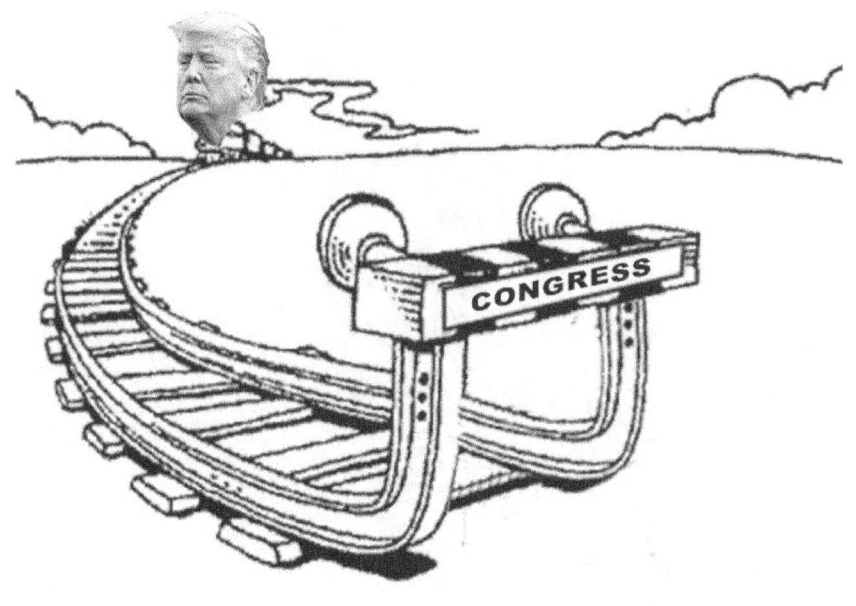

**Democratic "do-nothing" CONgress
is a break on the way of the President's progress.**

Trump: "My way or highway".

**Speaker Pelosi: "Go, make my day,
for your way you will quite dearly pay".**

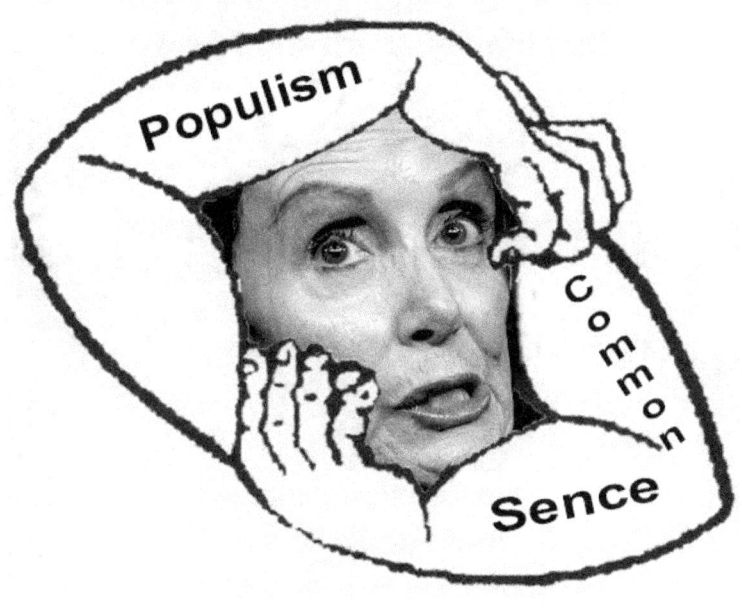

There is no manure in the world
that would not consider itself a fertilizer.

**Very often Mr. Schumer and speaker Pelosi
even good intentions are leveled out
by bad decisions.**

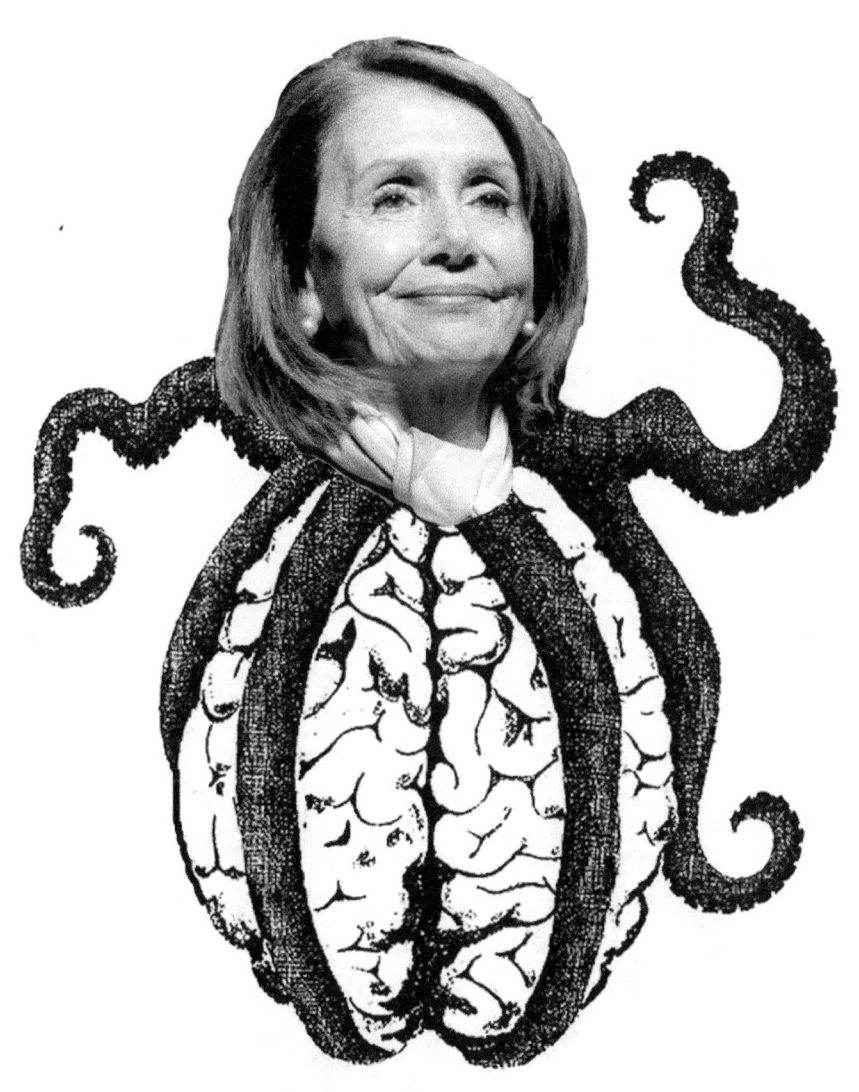

**Like cancer which must be radically treated
before it metastases spread,
the roots of evil impudent lie must be pulled out
before they will contaminate our society.**

Even those who ascended so high
that they achieved an orbit
still are vulnerable
to the gravitational pull of satire.

**That's how President Donald J. Trump
reacts to impeachment
from the *CON*gressional swamp.**

**Trump's kick in the ass
for Elizabeth Warren
is a way to progress.**

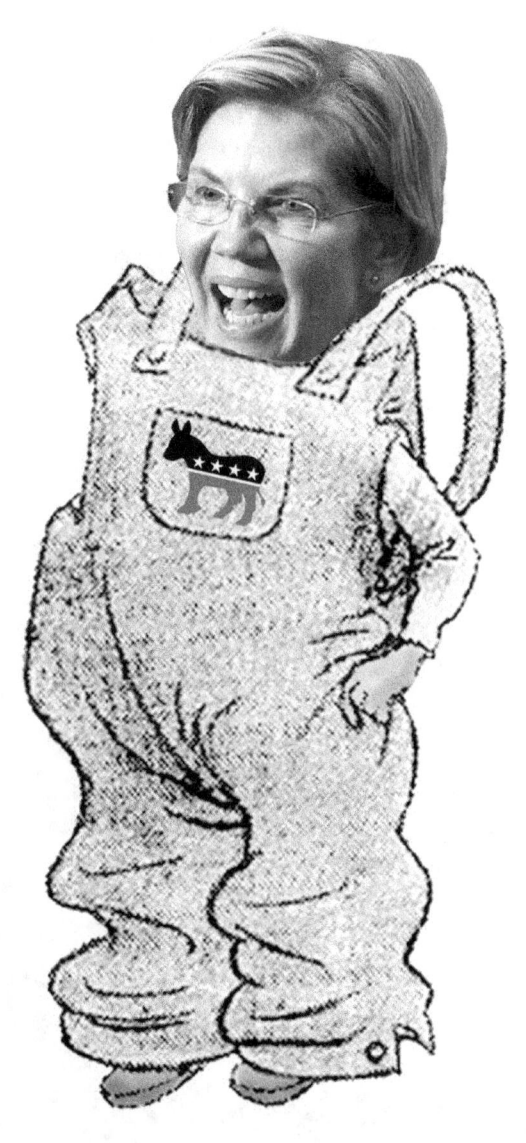

Toxic Warren:
"I am perfectly fit
for a presidential outfit."

HELLary is trying to sell people
her outdated ideas.
Unfortunately, they are not very fresh,
and who will trust a dealer
with second-hand goods?

HELLary is trying to convince people
that the socialist dirt
she is constantly dumping on America
would have healing power.

Before listening *HELL*ary
use a deodorant and take a painkiller.

***HELL*ary speech reminds**
of what gushes out of a broken sewer pipe.

"HELLary is not the solution
to our problems.
HELLary is the problem."
Paraphrased from Ronald Reagan.

Doctor who promise to heal our political system
thinks himself to be a surgeon,
but he is only a pathologist.

Satire is a judgement without right to objection.
It's Average Joe complete and final rejection.

**A limited brain can produce
an unlimited quantity of bullsh*t.**

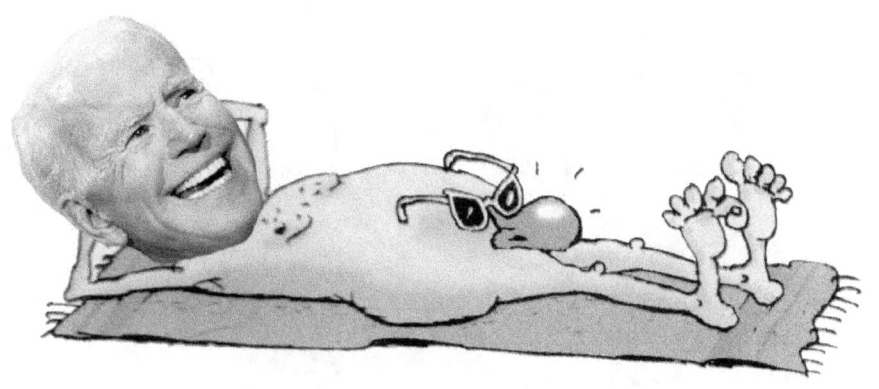

God gave average Joe two heads,
but blood to activate only one.
Guess which one.

Average Joe possesses only one wrinkle of wisdom,
on which he sits on.

Average Joe is like a noodle.
He's always in hot water and lacks taste.

Average Joe likes to work,
but only with pork.

**Average Joe cares about people
as a train cares about somebody it runs over.**

Jingle bell, Jingle bell,
corrupted Joe Biden, go to hell!

**Crazy Joe is one of those bad things
what sometimes happen to good people.**

People, beware of the person
who constantly talks about his high morality.
He may steal from you.

Average Joe will soon announce
that he is not interested in being the President.
The coronation ceremony
is scheduled for April 1st.

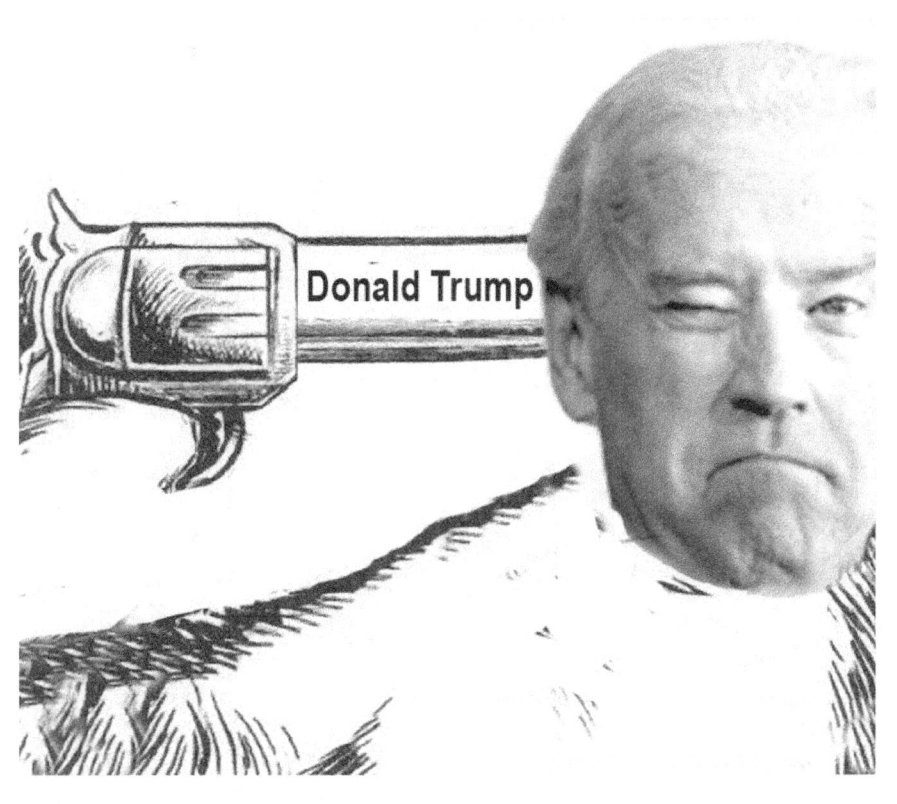

Donald Trump

Average Joe soon announced his resignation
due to fatigue.
"What fatigue?"
Because his constituents said
that they got very tired him.

It's better to vote for the ass of an elephant than for the head of a donkey.

Whoever helps a smiling donkey today, tomorrow will be kissing its tail.

**Crazy Bernie is the best person
with the worst qualities to rule our country.**

If Crazy Bernie is the progressive brain of our nation, then why it smells so bad?

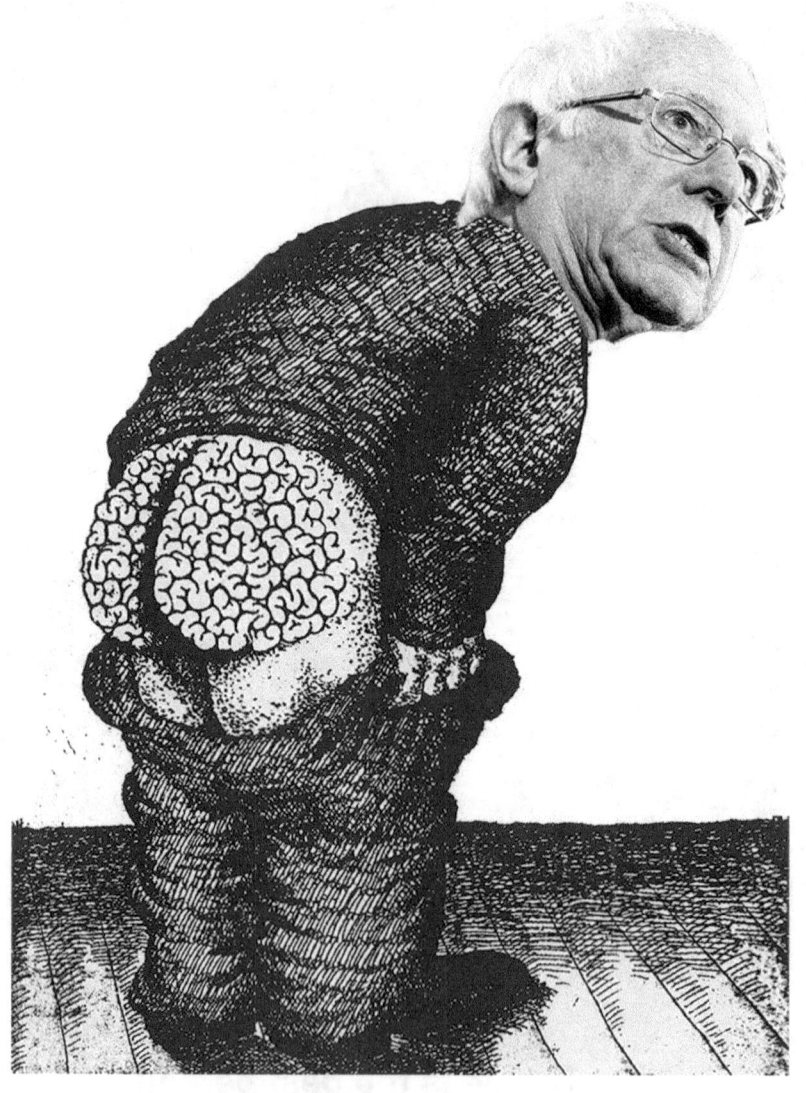

Old socialist possess only one wrinkle of wisdom, on which he sits on.

**Crazy Bernie's governing ability
is on the level of incurable cynility.**

**Crazy Bernie socialist transformation
is an existential threat to our nation.**

**Democratic *"hoaxful"*-frontrunner
keeps mentally challenged AOC as a banner.**

Crazy Bernie's dreams:
to retire on AOC attractive knees.

AOC delusional dream:
to become a VP supreme.
If Crazy Sanders will get a fatal heart attack,
AOC will jump in a chair of a disabled shmuck.

It's a socialist mental pollution.
AOC is able to conduct only sex-revolution.

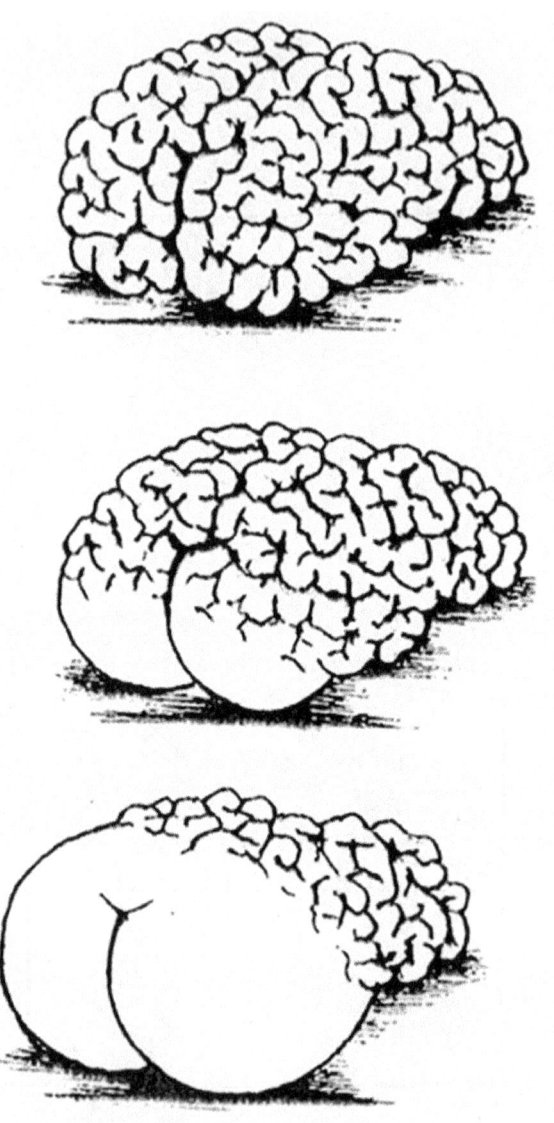

**Lawmaker Mrs. Ocasio Cortez
brains evolution is in certain progress
with appearance of uneducated
but very attractive ass.**

Everything free is only in a trap,
but deplorables trust AOC stupid crap.

AOC is a lollipop that one can lick
for a long time but it is better to spit it out.

**People don't see what they like
and don't like what they see.**

**Mr. Bloomberg is not a Republican
and not a Democrat
he is a political weathervane,
rustless opportunist and bureaucrat.**

Everybody know that Michael Bloomberg
sits on a giant pile of money,
but we also know
on what place he sits, set and will sit.

Mike Bloomberg:
"Of cause ideas are good
but money are good always.
Money can turn ideas into reality"

Mike Bloomberg feel himself
as captain of powerful ship sailing to success.

Unfortunately it could be ship of fools.

**If the White House is for sale
billionaire Michael Bloomberg will do prevail.**

Donald Trump is able to tear down
his contender apart.
And put what is left
into a museum of Surrealistic Art.

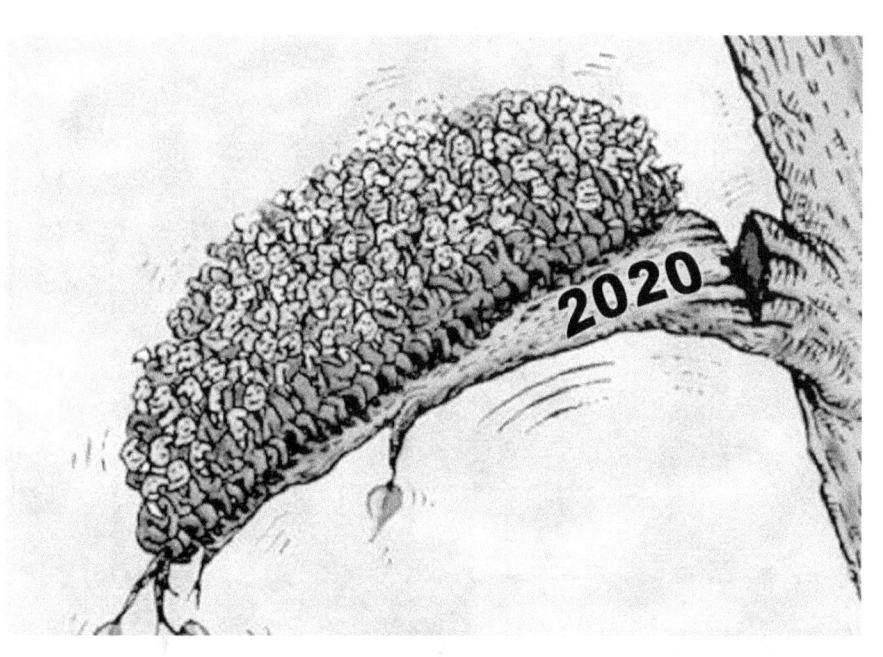

Satirical Champ, Professor KATZ foreses precipice for democ*RAT*s.

Donald Trump's God's Blessed mission is rotten socialism demolition.

Trump to Democrats:
"You voted for my impeachment,
so congratulations,
but I can't help you in this situation".

Donald Trump refused sings
together with democratic bunch of penguins.

**It's not the second opinion or guess,
Trump perfectly handles impeachment crap
from *CON*gress.**

President:
"Our "do-nothing" CONgress needs reconstruction,
let's start this necessary action."

Trump's platoon will be not overrun
by ugly delusional democratic sham.

**Unbeatable Trump's elephant army
is on the march.
Soon they will be honored
in the Washington victory arch.**

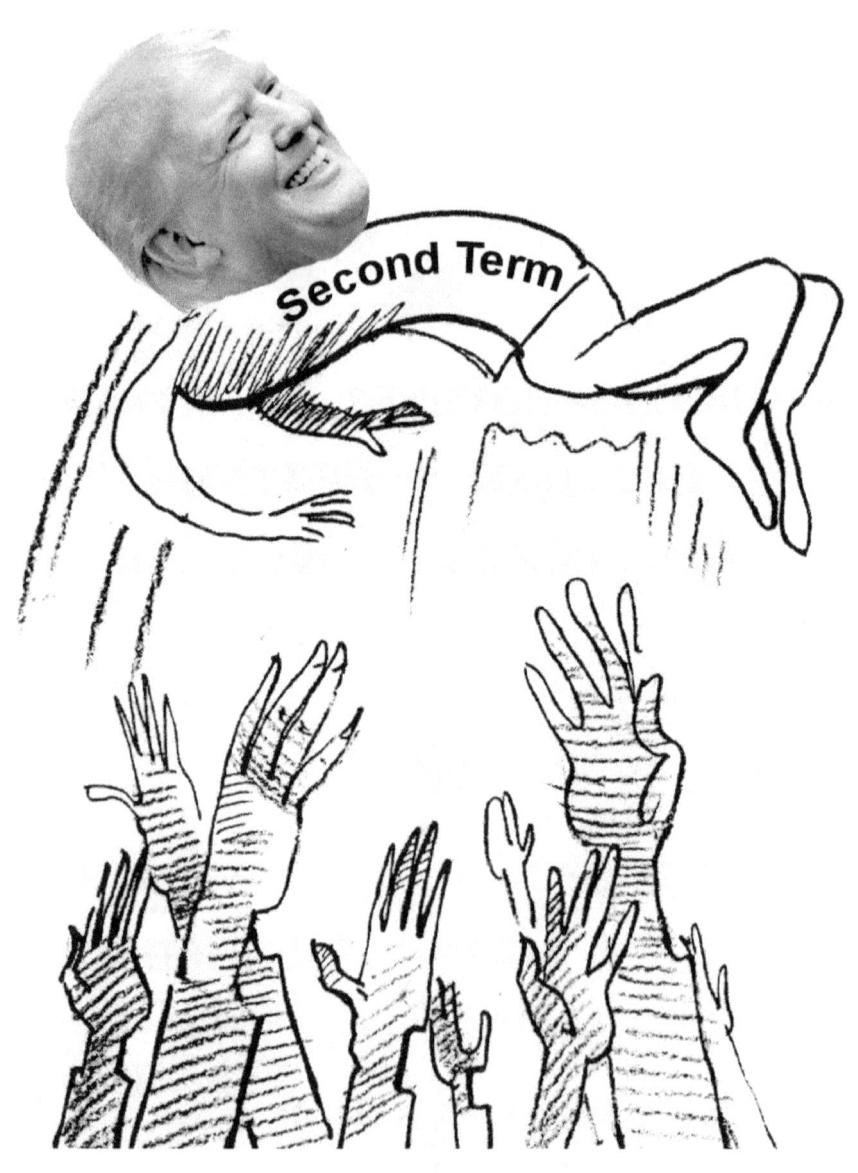

"Cult" of Trump beats cult of socialism, which is a cult of kleptocracy and bureaucratism.

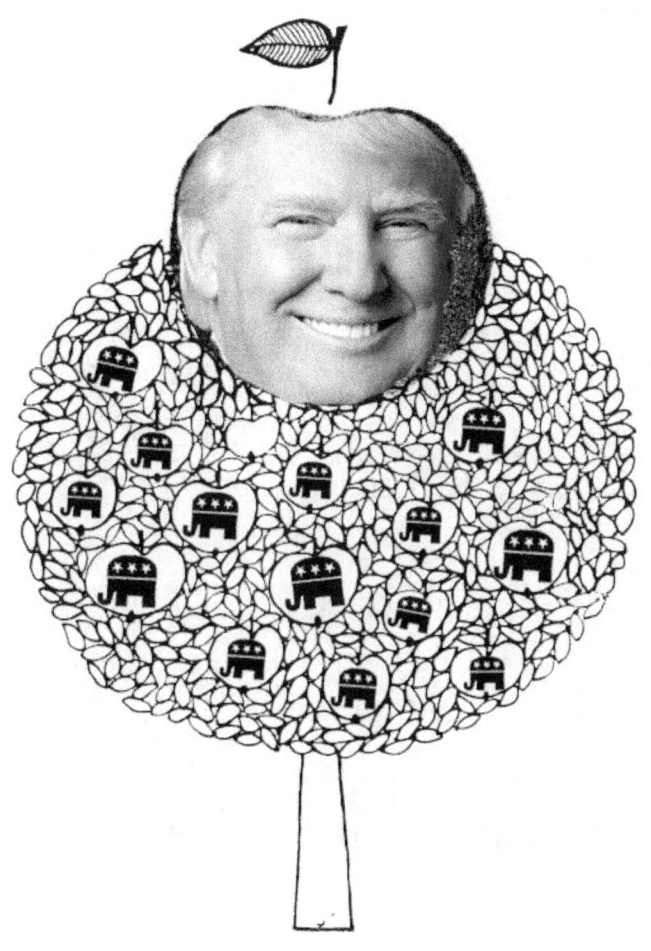

America expect
from the New Republican Congress
the real great progress.

Donald Trump will not vacate a White House.
Place of glory is not for socialist Mickey Mouse.

**If we are attacked by Democrats from the left,
we'll respond with a blow from the right.
If they attack us below the belt,
we'll attack even lower.**

When our President reads a sermon world listens.

Trump can talk peace, but not on his knees.

To hit or not to hit,
Trump never will accept retreat.

**America needs the very strong fist
to protect population from terrorists.**

When Iranian Super terrorist was shown
his real face,
normal citizens screamed in fear.

**Who has God on his lips,
sometimes has Devil in his heart.**

**General Soleimani swore on Koran
to keep pledge of allegiance
to bombs, rockets and guns.**

General Suleimani: "Death, go to my ass!"
Death: "Ok, you will get rectum cancer!"

General Soleimani: "I have a brave heart,
and don't respect your crazy fart."
Death: "Ok, you will have a fatal drone attack,
take it easy, don't behave as a schmuck."

*"Let's Iran disappear in flames
but great islam will prosper forever".*

- Father of islamic nation of Iran

Ayatollah Ruhollah Khomeini

Sometimes people fall in love
with their charismatic, delusional,
emotional, compulsive leader
and such obsession always leads to disaster.

Trump is winning over Iran.
Terrorists are on the run.

EMP is not a fantasy or abstraction.
EMP is a weapon of existential mass destruction.

We need immediate protection
from strike of EMP.
In reality it's *"To be, or not to be"*

To keep producing outdated military merchandise is not so wise.

Trump's executive order on "Coordinating National Resilience to Electromagnetic Pulses" will make him the President-Defender of whole Nation and Saver of American civilisation.

Doctor Trump, please,
protect country's electric power grid's health
against EMP, which could destroy
our Motherland well-being and wealth.

People, be aware and prepare.
Iran promises us a nightmare.

America is under threat of an EMP attack.
Unfortunately we are not prepared to act.

North Korea, Russia, China and Iran
are American enemies and it's not fun.

EMP could our Motherland mercilessly hit because CONgress is engaged in bullsh@t.

All things are possible except skiing through a revolving door. Who needs to be a winner in a nuclear war?

President is boomerang on Iranian lie.
He declares: "I am ready to fly".

**We need against EMP immediate protection.
It will be a major point of Trump's reelection.**

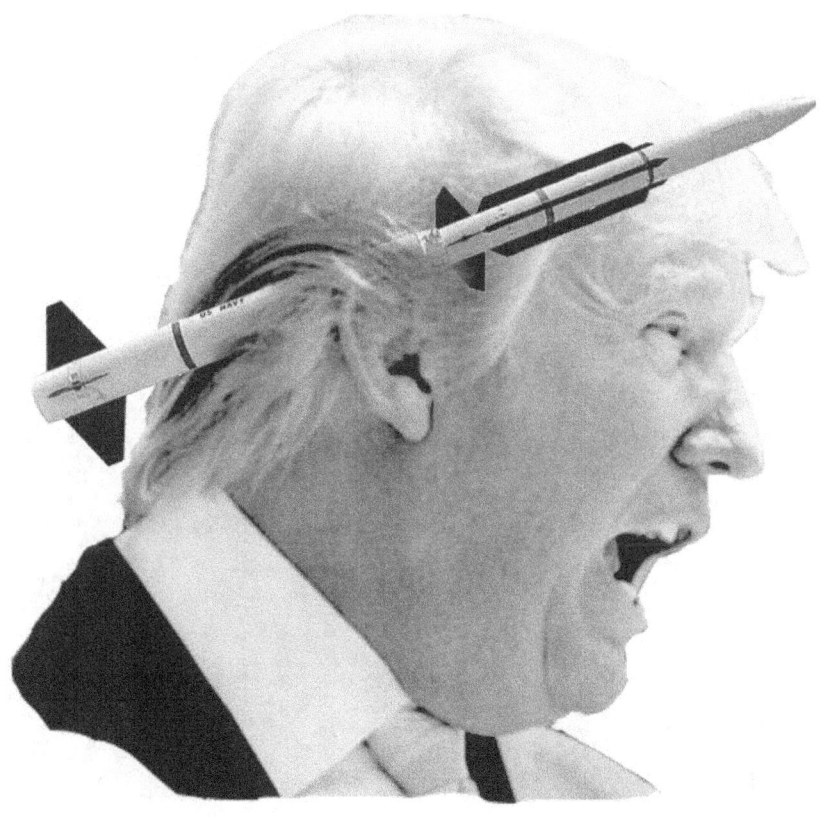

**If we don't drastically improve
homeland security today,
it will be our headache tomorrow.**

**What's the difference between Crazy Kim
and a pit bull?
Crazy Kim should never be unleashed.**

**Crazy Kim is like an animal, messy,
insensitive and potentially violent.
But according to Trump
he does make a funny pet.**

Melania is the best soldier in Trump's Army.

**Melania: "I am proud to live
at the same time as my husband".**

Trump:
"I love you and you love me.
We'll remain the First Family".

Author is not a Nostradamus,
just *KATZ*stradamus.

But he foresees that in 2024,
America will have a new President-Ivanka Trump,
who will continue to attack bureaucratic swamp.

America needs woman-President
because women smarter than men.
Where you can see a woman
who will lose her mind
because her colleague possess beautiful legs.

**"Per aspera, ad astra" (Latin),
"Trough the thorns, to the stars".**

**I am a daughter of the victorious dad.
Everything I want, I will be able to get.**

**Let American prosperity grow up
under the leadership
of President Donald J. Trump.**

Make your wish come true America.
Of course, our famous Santa Trumpus
will win over democratic contender Mickey Mouse.

"We, the People" will stay
with Liberty and Constitution.
That's why we support
President Trump's revolution.

The author was invited to Reagan's inauguration. Hopefully, Donald Trump also will honor satirist with an invitation.

**If you want to make America great again
please send your contribution
to continue Trump's revolution.**